Fizz&Martina™

in

The Incredible
Not-For-Profit Pet Resort Mystery™

Written and illustrated
by Peter Reynolds

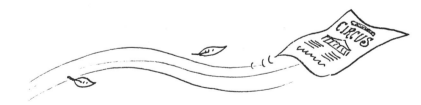

Tom Snyder Productions

Special thanks to
Peggy Healy Stearns,
Bruce Michael Green, and Tom Snyder.

Additional thanks to
Laurie Bennett, Annette Cate, Annette Donnelly,
Maura Dwyer, Laurel Kayne, Janet Reynolds, and Matt Smith.

Published by Tom Snyder Productions
80 Coolidge Hill Road, Watertown, MA 02172-2817, USA

Printed in the United States of America.
ISBN 1-55998-436-8

First printing, 1993.

CONTENTS

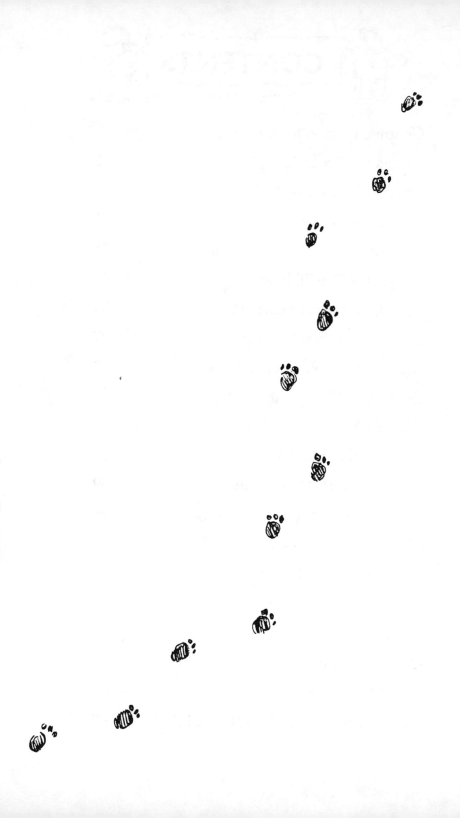

To my daughter, Sarah.

Chapter One
Open for Business

Rain had been soaking the town of Blue Falls for nearly a week. Dark clouds, heavy rains, lightning and thunder, all made the town feel rather creepy. On the north side of town, along the Blue Falls River, an old hotel stood bravely against the storm. The rain was coming down so hard that it was difficult to read the newly painted sign hanging outside on the front lawn.

BOOM! The thunder cracked loudly, waking Fizz from his nap.

"Fizz, are you sleeping on the job again?" Martina snapped. "It doesn't help business for customers to walk in with you snoring."

"Martina, I'm sorry," Fizz yawned before saying,"but does it really matter? I mean, we had our grand opening four days ago and *nobody* has walked through the door."

"Fizz, Fizz, Fizz," Martina sighed. "Of course it matters, this weird rain is keeping all our customers away and besides— you just *can't* sleep on the job, no matter *who* doesn't come through that door. What if firefighters slept on the job?"

"They do, Martina. A bunch of them sleep while one of them sits by the telephone waiting for it to ring. That's like us. I sleep. You stay by the phone."

"Oh, brother," Martina sighed as she sat down next to Fizz who was slumped over the reception desk.

"Anyway, Martina, you're better at handling emergencies. I always get nervous and confused."

"Fizz, this isn't a 911 Emergency Center we're running here. It's a pet resort. Martina and Fizz's Incredible Not-For-Profit Pet Resort."

"Uh, actually, it's *Fizz* and Martina's Incredible Not-For-Profit Pet Resort."

"Says who?"

"The sign outside says so."

Martina peered out the office window at the storm outside. "Fizz, the rain has washed off all the paint."

"Oh. Maybe I shouldn't have used watercolors," he said softly.

"Okay, forget the sign. We have work to do. One of us has to go feed the animals. The other has to do some marketing."

"I already picked up the animal food at the market last night," Fizz reminded Martina.

"Fizz, not that kind of marketing! I mean the business kind of marketing. Like taking surveys and making graphs and stuff to find out what our customers want. Then we use that information to improve our services so more customers will patronize us. And that will make our pet resort a big hit and make *us* happy."

"Uncle Q says I patronize him, but it doesn't seem to make him happy," said Fizz.

"That's a *different* kind of patronizing."

"Wow, Martina. How can you keep track of all those words? You're pretty smart."

"I read, Fizz. I READ *everything* I can get my hands on. While you sleep, I read. I'll take care of the marketing. You go feed our friends. I think they're all in the Health Club."

Fizz got up, stretched his arms and yawned. Martina picked up the phone and dialed. It rang and then she heard someone on the other end of the phone say "Hello?"

"Good afternoon, sir. I am Martina of Martina and Fizz's Pet Resort. I'd like to ask you a few questions for our pet survey." She picked up her pencil and got ready to write on her survey sheet.

"I'm not interested. I don't care WHAT you're selling. I don't want any!" the man on the phone yelled. He sounded very upset.

"Sir, I'm not selling anything right now. I'm just interested in what your favorite animal is," Martina said hopefully.

"Okay, kid. My favorite animal is a click."

"What's a click, sir?" Martina asked.

"*This* is a click. . . ." CLICK! The man had hung up the phone.

Martina smiled. Hanging up on someone is

rude, but she always appreciated a clever joke.

"Maybe I'd better do the favorite animal survey with someone I *know*." She dialed carefully. "Hi, Mom? It's me. What's your favorite animal?"

Her mom said, "You, Martina. You're my favorite animal."

"Funny, Mom. Real funny. Everybody's a joker today."

After an hour or so of calls, Martina looked at her survey sheet. Seven people had said that dogs were their favorite animals. Three said cats. Two said rabbits. Martina realized that maybe their resort needed more dogs. At the moment they only had Fizz's and Budge's dogs.

Martina got up and walked to the window. The stormy sky looked like a Fourth of July fireworks show seen on a black and white TV.

"It may not matter *how* many dogs we have at this resort if this rain doesn't stop. This whole place could slide into the Blue Falls River."

A flash of lightning lit up the sky as Martina closed the curtains.

11

Chapter 2
Poolside

Fizz walked down the quiet hall until he came
to the Health Club. As he opened the door, the
noise grew louder. Quacking, music, oinking,
laughter, chirping, bouncing balls, barking, weights
clanking, meowing and a symphony of other
sounds mingled together.

A cat walked between Fizz's legs with her eyes
closed without saying a word. "Cats are so moody"
Fizz thought.

He walked to the edge of the pool. Three goldfish swam rapidly towards him. They were happy
to see Fizz. Sammy, the biggest fish, jumped into
the air.

"Afternoon, Fizz! You look tired." Sammy splashed back into the pool.

The second fish jumped into the air and said, "When will the guests start coming, Fizz?" And SPLASH! Tammy was back in the pool.

Fizz wiped his face dry and peered back into the pool. The smallest goldfish poked his little face above the water. "I'm too little to jump and talk at the same time, Fizz, but I'm light enough to float and talk."

Fizz smiled at Tony.

"Fizz?" Tony asked after he swam a circle around his brother and sister. "Tammy and Sammy say that this pet resort idea is a flop. They say nobody wants to pay money to take a vacation with a talking animal."

"Nobody's going to believe you, Fizz," barked Scamper. Fizz looked up to see his dog Scamper wearing a pair of goggles.

"What are the goggles for, Scamper?"

"They protect my eyes when I play racquetball."

"I didn't know you played." Fizz looked surprised. He took off his sneakers and dipped his feet into the pool as Scamper plopped down next to him.

"I *don't* know how to play, Fizz. Laurel, the squirrel monkey, is giving me lessons. I'm trying to be prepared for the guests when — *if* they come."

Fizz said, "They'll come. Martina's doing a pet survey as we speak. She says it'll help business.

She'll make a graph and post it in the lobby for everyone to see."

Fizz pulled a warm baloney sandwich from his jacket. He slipped out the baloney for Scamper. He crumpled up the bread for Sammy, Tammy and Tony, who were tickling his toes in the water. "I really hope the pet resort catches on. I like it here. This could be the best summer in the history of Blue Falls."

"If it ever stops raining," Scamper growled slowly as he pulled the baloney string off of his baloney.

BOOM! They heard another clap of thunder. Laurel swung over to the window from the light fixtures. She looked out at the black sky. Rain pounded against the window. Fizz walked over to Laurel. He was followed by Scamper and Budge's dog, Flat Top, Virginia's two cats, Mildred and Crumpet, and finally, Martina's bunny, Carl.

"Looks bad," Laurel squealed in her high, squirrel monkey voice. "Reeeeaal bad. Something's creeeeeeeeeeepy about this weatherrrr. Don't like it. Don't like it one bit. Got a bad feeeling, I do. Bad feeeling. Bad."

With those words, the room went silent. Laurel was usually right about things. Fizz hoped she wasn't right this time.

BOOM!

Chapter 3
The Circus Sloshes to Town

What's the worst storm you've ever seen? Have you ever seen it rain so hard that you couldn't see five inches in front of your face? Have you ever seen it so heavy that the windshield wipers of your car don't do a lick of good? Have you ever walked through torrents so heavy that you could hardly keep your eyes open? Have you. . . okay, you get my point. THAT kind of storm is the storm that broke loose at the end of that rainy week in Blue Falls. Just when people were saying: "This has *got* to be the end of it! There couldn't possibly be a drop left to drop from the sky." How wrong they were.

On that Sunday afternoon, the biggest part of the storm broke loose. It was the kind of storm where it rains so hard you can't see five inches in front of your face. It was the kind of storm. . . oh. Okay, I think I've already said that. Anyway, it was a doozy of a storm.

At noon on that torrential day, a strange sight appeared on the road above Blue Falls Ridge. Lightning lit up the sky in a mean horizontal streak. Then, it went dark.

FLASH! Again the lightning tore across the stormy sky. Thunder erupted like an angry bear roaring among the dark clouds.

I don't think there's been a scarier day in Blue Falls. I say "day" because it *was* day. It was high noon, but the storm had swallowed the sun.

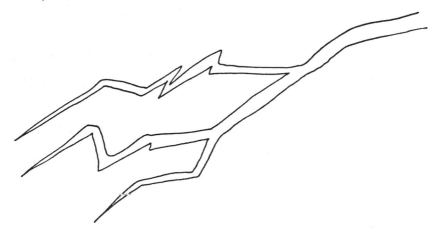

People wondered if it still existed. It was high noon, but it *looked* like midnight.

If you looked carefully, every time the lightning bolted overhead, you may have seen the strange caravan that had come to a muddy stop above Blue Falls. If you had been able to see through the heavy rain, you would have seen a dirty, rusty truck struggling to pull several cages behind it. The thick, hungry mud made it difficult for the wheels to grip the road, to move closer to Blue Falls.

If the thunder hadn't been so loud, you would have heard the terrible laughter and the terrible words coming from the man in the ratty old top hat. You would have seen his evil face. His sharp wiry whiskers. His badly scratched hands on the steering wheel of the whining truck. You would have seen the rusty cages being pulled behind. The sad eyes of the wet horses. The hungry faces of the monkeys. The tears of the old elephant. You would have seen the terrible circus that was about to make Blue Falls its home.

CRACK!!! BOOM!! The thunder and lightning cried. But you couldn't see any of this. It was too dark.

The lights in the pet resort office flickered on and off and on again. The storm was getting worse. Martina picked up her pet survey and stuffed it into her backpack. Fizz was waiting by the front door.

"How did the survey go, Martina?"

"Okay, I guess, but the phone stopped working. I think the storm knocked out the phone lines. I'll make more calls tomorrow. I've called most of my friends. Maybe I could call some of your friends tomorrow, Fizz?"

"Well, you'll be talking to yourself. You're really the only friend I've made here. I mean, I *know* a lot of kids, grown-ups too, but Martina, you're the only *real* friend I have."

Martina wasn't sure whether she should frown or smile. The sound of her dad's station wagon interrupted them. HONK! HONK!

"Quick, Fizz. Let's go!"

As they ran to the car, Fizz yelled, "Will the pets be okay tonight?"

"Relax, Fizz. It's just rain. They're all safe and sound."

Fizz tried to relax as they drove off slowly through the murky night.

Chapter 4

Out of Breath

The next day surprised everyone in Blue Falls. The rain, the wind, the thunder had all stopped. There it was. The sun. That wonderful yellow ball floating in the beautiful blue sky. It was weird how the storm had vanished and had been replaced by one of those magically perfect summer days. Not too hot. Slightly breezy. Green. Blue. Yellow. If only everything that happened that day could have been so lovely.

"Uncle Q! Uncle Q!" Fizz burst through the door, panting like a dog. "You won't. . . you won't . . . you won't believe this. . . I can't. . . I can't. . . believe it. . . my. . . myself. . . ."

Uncle Quesmit adjusted his baseball cap and turned slowly to look at his nephew.

"It must be actually important," thought Uncle Q. Fizz knew not to talk to his uncle during any televised sporting event. Uncle Quesmit had the 24 Hour Sports Galore Channel, so it *always* seemed that Fizz was interrupting him.

Fizz's mouth was now moving, but no words came out. He was completely out of breath. Uncle Q decided to take a guess at what his nephew was miming wildly.

"Yeah, the rain stopped. I know, Fizzmond. Big deal. I was kinda gettin' to like it. If only Dingers Stadium had a retractable roof, now *that* would be. . . ."

Then Uncle Q jumped from his chair when he saw Fizz had fallen to the floor! It was rare that anyone could get Uncle Q out of his chair while he was watching TV, but Fizz had managed to do it.

Uncle Q ran over and grabbed hold of Fizz. He noticed tears rolling down Fizz's face. Fizz was trying to say something. Uncle Q wasn't big on hugs, but he knew Fizz needed one.

"C'mon Fizz. Take it easy, sport. Breathe. Take a breath, will ya?" Uncle Q had seen some of his players like this after being hit in the stomach by a fastball. Actually, it looked like Fizz was hurt worse.

"Scamp," Fizz managed to say through his tears. "He. . . He's gone. He's. . . ."

22

"Calm down, Fizz," consoled Uncle Q. "I told you that resort for animals was a wacky idea. Scamper probably thought it was dumb, too, and decided to take a hike."

"No! Uncle Q, he. . . . he was excited about the club. He. . . he. . . was taking racquetball lessons from the squirrel monkey."

"Have you been playing the outfield, son?"

"Please, believe me," Fizz managed a complete sentence. His breath had slowed to a heavy pant.

"This afternoon I found muddy footprints in the hallway of the resort. Tony, the goldfish, thought he heard Scamp howling. All I found in the hall were muddy shoe prints and a long, wiry whisker." Fizz held the whisker between his plump fingers. "It's not from an animal, sir. I just know it."

Uncle Q stared at it. "Well, kid. If it's from a human being, I'd be surprised. But you're right. It's not from an animal."

Uncle Q was worried but tried not to show it. He thought that maybe he could calm Fizz down by reminding him of the time the Chinook was lost.

"Remember, little buddy? We were all goin' nuts lookin' for that little Chinook fella, but we pulled together and found him." Uncle Q looked hopefully at Fizz. Fizz managed a smile, not because of the Chinook story, but because Uncle Q was being so nice to him. He wondered if Uncle Q would call him "little buddy" on a more regular basis. Fizz suddenly felt hopeful.

"Anything's possible, Uncle Q. And if anything's possible, maybe we will find Scamper."

Chapter 5

The Station and the Scoop

The sun was shining on Blue Falls. Uncle Q drove his red sports car down Route 9. He was very pleased to be driving again after a long, rainy week. His car had no roof, so he hadn't been able to take it out on the road.

He pulled into the Blue Falls Police Station parking lot, carefully navigating his way around all the leftover rain puddles. The storm had been gone for a whole day but the town was still a soggy mess. Fizz and Martina undid their seat belts when the car came to a full stop. Fizz noticed that Uncle Q had parked in a spot with a sign that said 'VIP Parking.'

"Uncle Q, what's vip parking?"

25

Martina chimed in, "Not vip, Fizz. V I P. Very Important Person." Uncle Q nodded in agreement as he strutted toward the door. Fizz noticed a water pump machine swooshing water out of the basement window of the station. "Looks like they're busy cleaning up after the storm. I hope the police have time to help us find Scamper," thought Fizz.

The police chief gave Uncle Q a big smile and a firm handshake as they all sat down in the office. The police hadn't always been this nice to Uncle Quesmit until he became owner of the Blue Falls baseball team, the Dingers, a few years earlier. Season tickets have a strange effect on people. Now they were all handshakes and pats on the back.

The chief looked over at Fizz and spoke slowly and seriously.

"Your uncle told me on the phone that Scamper is missing. Son, as you probably have noticed, we're very busy trying to set things right after the storm nearly washed us all away. The traffic lights are still broken. Blue Falls bridge is badly damaged. . . . The point is, Fizzmond, that we're very tied up at the moment. If it weren't for the fact that your uncle is such an important person in Blue Falls, I wouldn't even have been able to see you at all today."

The chief glanced at Uncle Q who was smiling ear to ear.

"The point is, son, a missing dog is a low priority for the police right now."

Fizz could feel his face getting warm and red.

He felt very helpless and a little bit mad.

"Well, ma'am, Scamper is a HIGH priority for ME!" Fizz surprised himself with how mad he sounded.

The police chief rolled her chair closer to Fizz. She said, "Low priority doesn't mean *no* priority. You tell me the story of how he got lost, and I promise we'll do our best to find Scamper as soon as we can."

Fizz looked over at Martina who gave him the two thumbs up sign.

"Okay, Fizz. Where was your dog last seen?"

"At the pet resort, sir, I mean, ma'am. Fizz and Martina's Incredible Not-For-Profit Pet Resort."

"Pet resort? What pet resort?" Chief Blinker asked.

"Martina, you'd better explain. She's better with words than me, your honor."

Martina stood up and then sat down. "You don't know about our pet resort, Chief? Gee, I guess our advertising needs work. Well, Fizz and I have turned my Uncle Zeek's hotel into a kind of pet store, but there are no cages, and people can't buy the animals. And it's part health spa. People can come relax with the animal of their choice. And the animals are free to come and go as they please."

The chief was listening carefully.

"It's a proven fact, " Martina continued, "that hanging around animals makes a person happier and calmer. The more relaxed you are— the easier it is to hear the animals when they talk to you."

Fizz noticed that Chief and Uncle Q both were trying not to laugh.

"You don't believe us, do you?" Martina said.

"I, well, I. . . . ah. I'm a bit confused. You mean the old abandoned hotel up by Blue Falls River? Hmmm. I forgot that it belonged to your uncle."

"When he left Blue Falls he gave it to Mom, but she's been too busy with her astronomy work to do anything with it, so Fizz and I decided to turn it into. . ."

Martina was interrupted when a police officer rushed into the office and said "Excuse me, Chief Blinker, but we've just got a call from Farmer Casey. He's all upset. Seems a circus has moved onto his field without his permission."

"Pardon me, we'll have to continue this later. I've got to go. We'll find Scraper, I promise."

"Scamper, sir, I mean ma'm," corrected Fizz, but Chief Blinker had run out the door.

On the way home, Uncle Q stopped at the ice cream parlor. It was crowded because this was the first day in a long time that actually felt like summer.

"Hi, Mr. Barney." Fizz thought it was weird to see his math teacher selling ice cream. It seemed to Fizz that teachers should have the summer off like kids did.

"What'll it be, folks?" Mr. Barney had his ice cream scoop at the ready.

"Make mine chocolate, Mr. B.," said Uncle Q.

"That's *definitely* a very popular flavor today, " Mr. Barney said.

"I'll have a vanilla, sir," Martina licked her lips.

"Another very popular flavor! I should take a survey sometime of the most popular flavors in Blue Falls," said their teacher.

"I'm doing a favorite *pet* survey for our pet resort. What's *your* favorite animal?"

Fizz interrupted Martina; he was starving.

"Excuse me. Mr. Barney? I'd like a cup of beef and baked bean ice cream, please."

They all looked at Fizz.

"I'm afraid that's not one of our top-selling flavors, Fizz."

"Okay, how 'bout hot dog and chocolate chip?"

"Sorry, Fizz. I don't have that one."

"Chicken and strawberry?"

"We *do* have strawberry."

Fizz settled for strawberry and they all went outside to eat their ice cream. They sat in the brilliant sunshine enjoying a little bit of new-found summer. The ice cream *had* helped to take Fizz's mind off Scamper, but not completely. He wondered if they would ever see him again.

Chapter 6

The Billboard

On Tuesday, Fizz and Martina met in town to do errands for the resort. Business had actually started picking up. Mr. Barney had stopped by to reserve a boat ride with Virginia's cats. A couple on their way through from Cherry Hill stopped in and reserved a room for a week. They had made plans to climb Blue Falls mountain with William, the mountain goat.

"What a beautiful day! This is *definitely* my favorite time of year! What's yours, Fizz?"

"Martina, I love *all* the seasons."

"You've *got* to have a favorite."

"Why do I have to have a favorite? What's all

this favorite stuff lately? Favorite pets. Favorite ice cream."

"Fizz, okay. Don't tell me your favorite season. I don't care."

Fizz pulled out a sandwich for them to share as they sat on a bench at the bus stop.

"Spring," Fizz said quietly.

"Spring what?" Martina asked.

"My favorite season."

Across the street they noticed a new billboard being painted. They watched as the painter finished. He adjusted his old top hat and disappeared over a fence.

The billboard showed a colorful circus. Fizz read the words on the sign:

"Opening this Saturday! Mr. Crumple's Wonder Circus. Come See the Happiest Animals on Earth!"

The painting of the animals showed monkeys and horses and a big elephant.

"Those animals don't look very happy to me, Fizz. Look. There are chains around their necks. There's *no way* I'm going to *that* circus. I have a bad feeling about it."

They walked over to the billboard. Smaller words explained that the circus was on Farmer Casey's farm.

"It couldn't be all bad, Martina. Farmer Casey loves animals. He'd never let a bad circus stay on his farm. Let's just go on Saturday to see what it's all about."

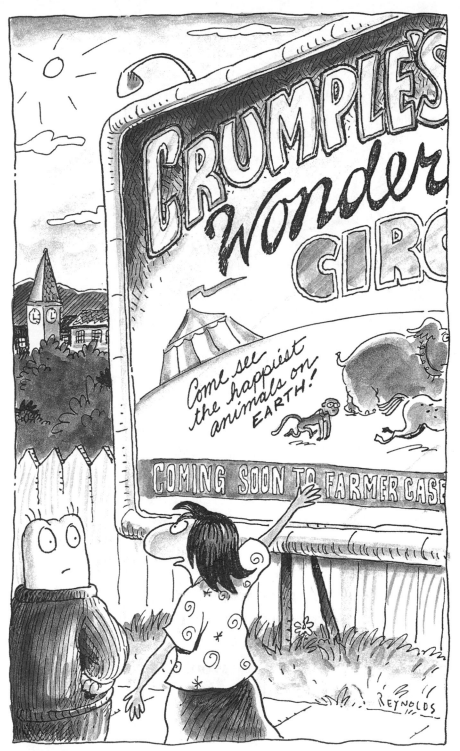

33

Chapter 7

Out of Breath Part 2

Saturday morning Fizz woke up later than he had planned, but he was very tired. It had been a busy week at the pet resort. He rolled over and looked at his alarm clock. Ten o'clock.

He quickly got dressed and went downstairs. Uncle Q was sitting in the big green armchair. He was already watching TV.

"Do you want to go to the circus today, Uncle Q?" Fizz said hopefully. He crossed his fingers. Maybe Uncle Quesmit would give him a ride to Farmer Casey's farm so he wouldn't be late. He had promised to meet Martina at eleven o'clock.

"I'm busy. There's a very important sports show on at noon."

Uncle Q handed Fizz the TV Guide and pointed to a picture of race cars going around a track.

"It's the Windy 2000 Tar Burner Road Race Spectacular. I wouldn't miss it if you paid me." He wasn't kidding.

"Uncle Q? Why do they call car racing a sport? It doesn't seem like a sport to me."

Uncle Q had stopped listening. Fizz decided to just get going as fast as he could.

Martina was relieved to see Fizz running up the hill to Farmer Casey's field. He was sweaty and out of breath. It was a very hot day.

"Take it easy, Fizz. You shouldn't run like that on such a hot day. Why didn't you get a ride from Uncle Q?"

Fizz was busy trying to catch his breath.

"Don't tell me—Uncle Q was too busy watching TV, right? Figures. I feel sorry for you, Fizz."

They started walking toward the circus gate. There were lots of people gathered around waiting to get in. When they finally opened the gates, everyone poured in. There were five big circus tents set up, a couple of rides, and some food stands.

Fizz and Martina saw a purple tent. There was a sign outside it which said "Only one dollar to see the strange Feathered Fargle! The only animal like it in the world!" There was a painting of this strange beast on the sign. It had four legs and golden feathers and a pair of wings. It had long floppy ears and little fangs.

"Save your money, Fizz. It's probably a puppet or something. These side show attractions are usually a rip-off."

"Martina, you're so cynical."

"Where did you learn the word cynical'?"

"From you, Martina."

"See! It pays off to hang out with me even if you don't understand what I'm saying half the time."

They moved on to the big yellow tent. They bought a ticket to see the animal show they had been hearing so much about. They wanted to see for themselves how the animals were being treated.

Chapter 8

Where's Trooper?

Warning: This chapter is scary.

Fizz led the way into the big, dark tent. There was a man wearing a top hat standing in the center of the circus ring lighting several torches. He had lit four and the flames were lashing about wildly, throwing light around the tent. Nearly two hundred people had squeezed onto the wooden benches set up around the circle. He lit the fifth, and the sixth, and finally the seventh torch.

"Seven torches, Martina. Seven is my unlucky number. I think something bad is going to happen," Fizz said as he tried to get comfortable on the narrow, splintery bench.

"I've never heard of an *un*lucky number, Fizz. How do you figure seven is unlucky?"

"Well, seven *used to* be my lucky number, but it never seemed to work, so I decided it must be my unlucky number."

Fizz realized that Martina wasn't listening. She had noticed that a big rusty cage with wheels was being pushed out into the ring. There were six horses inside the cage barely able to move.

"Welcome to Crumple's Wonder Circus Animal Show!" The man in the hat shouted. He wore a blue velvet suit that looked very dirty and old. His face was a greenish-yellow color with a few black, wiry whiskers curled into strange shapes.

He pulled a long whip off the ground and snapped it. The cage door slid open and the horses jumped out. They were dirty too, like Mr. Crumple's coat. They didn't seem as happy as he did, though. He snapped the whip near their hooves and they began running around him in circles. As they ran, another rusty cage was lowered from the ceiling, but this one was small. When it was in reach, Mr. Crumple opened the door and pulled a little monkey out of the cage. It was dressed in a clown costume and its face was painted like a clown too.

The crowd cheered and laughed which made Martina very angry.

"I don't get it, Fizz! Why are they laughing?

Can't they see that these animals need our help?
Look at those collars around the horses' necks.
They're way too tight!"

"I don't know why nobody else notices, Martina. Maybe they've never thought about animals'
feelings before. If they spent some time at our pet
resort they'd change their minds pretty fast."

Martina cringed when she saw Mr. Crumple throw the monkey into the air like a ball. Fortunately, the little monkey landed on top of a horse. He rode around the ring barely able to hang on.

Again the crowd cheered.

"What's *wrong* with these people? I guess it's going to be up to us to rescue these animals from Mr. Crumple."

"Uh, Martina? That Crumple guy looks kind of mean. Maybe we should go talk to Chief Blinker about this."

"Let's go outside and think of a plan. This place is making me mad," Martina said as she pushed her way through the crowd.

Outside they saw Farmer Casey scratching his head. They walked over to him. He looked worried.

"What's wrong, Farmer Casey?" asked Fizz.

"Well, golly, kids. I'm just feelin' awful. First this Mr. Crumple moves onto my land. . . "

"Why'd you let him?" Martina waited impatiently for an answer. Farmer Casey seemed to be thinking hard.

"Well, he promised me half the money he makes this month. That sounded like a lot of money. My barn needs fixin' pretty bad, so I said okay.

But I just don't trust this fellow."

"Have you seen the way his animals are treated?" asked Fizz.

"No, he keeps them locked up and he says I can't see the animal show due to something he calls 'conflict of interest.'"

Big drops of sweat were pouring off Farmer Casey's forehead. He said, "And now I can't find my horse, Trooper! Have you seen him?"

Martina and Fizz looked at each other.

"Scamper and now Trooper? What's going on around here, Fizz?"

"Weird, Martina. Very, very weird."

Chapter 9
Cooking Up a Plan

Martina got that crazy look in her eyes. One of her eyes looked angry and the other was excited. She started to run. Fizz and Farmer Casey tried to keep up with her.

Fizz yelled, "Where are you going?"

"I'm going to find Trooper! I have a feeling he's in one of those tents!!"

"Oh, dear!" Farmer Casey gasped, "Do you *really* think Mr. Crumple would try to steal Trooper?"

They followed Martina and ducked into a green tent. They looked around. Just a few rusty cages and a greasy popcorn machine.

Fizz rubbed his chin. "Hey! Maybe Mr. Crumple

42

put him in that horse show we saw. Maybe he painted over the black diamond shape on Trooper's nose."

Farmer Casey smiled broadly. "Fizz, you're brilliant." They poured out of the tent. As they passed a yellow tent, Farmer Casey stopped suddenly. He thought he had heard a horse whinny.

"Trooper?!" They ran into the tent and found Trooper tied to a pole.

Martina was furious. "Wait until Chief Blinker hears about this! She should come right away and take Mr. Crumple to jail. I had a feeling he stole your horse, Farmer Casey."

A soft, but greasy voice said, "Oh, *there* you are!" Everyone looked around, including Trooper, at a man standing in the doorway. He adjusted his top hat and dusted off his blue velvet coat.

Before anyone could say a word, Mr. Crumple went over to Trooper, patted him on his nose, and said in a warm voice, "Dear, me. I was *so* worried about your horse. I saw him wandering around the field. He looked thoroughly lost, so I took him in here and tied him up. I was looking *everywhere* for you. I *do* hope you weren't too worried."

"Well, I, um, well. . .   thank you, Mr. Crumple," Farmer Casey said sheepishly.

Then Mr. Crumple took out a handful of money and stuffed it in Farmer Casey's hands.

"This is half the money from today's show, like I promised." Mr. Crumple's voice was as soft as the velvet coat he wore.

Farmer Casey smiled and said. "Gee whiz, Mr. Crumple, sir. That's real nice of you. Real nice. Thanks for finding Trooper for me." Farmer Casey looked over at Fizz and Martina and stopped smiling. "These kids had me thinking that . . . "

Martina wisely interrupted, "Ah, well, Fizz and I are late. Gotta go. Come on, Fizz." She pushed Fizz out of the tent.

"Wow. I guess we were letting our imaginations run wild, Martina."

"Let's just go, Fizz."

"Just goes to show that you can't go accusing people of stuff unless you know the facts," said Fizz. Martina wasn't listening to Fizz. She was too busy thinking as fast as she was running.

The next day Fizz walked out of the pet resort onto the front lawn. He was carrying lemonade. A couple of the animals followed him.

"Martina, take a break." He put the tray down. "How's the sign coming?"

Martina put down her brush and stepped down the ladder. Fizz was surprised to see that she had put his name first on the sign. It read:

FIZZ AND MARTINA'S
INCREDIBLE PET RESORT

"Martina, I thought you wanted to call it *Martina and Fizz's Pet Resort.*"

"I figured it would cheer you up. Hey, what are friends for?" Martina took a glass of cold lemonade from Laurel the squirrel monkey.

Fizz read a small sign hanging from the big sign: NO VACANCY.

"Martina, what's a 'vacancy'? I mean, maybe we shouldn't tell people we don't have one. Maybe we should *buy* one for the resort."

Martina let Fizz finish rambling. "Fizz, NO VACANCY means there are no rooms left in our resort."

"Oh."

Martina took another sip of lemonade. "Can you believe how busy we've been lately? It's great."

Their friend, Skrimp, ran across the lawn. He held a backpack and a tennis racquet.

"No vacancy. Sorry, Skrimp." Fizz sounded very serious.

"Hi, guys. No, I don't need a room. I'm going to summer camp. I just wanted to say 'bye' before I left. The bus is picking me up across the street in ten minutes."

Fizz watched quietly. Skrimp began juggling four tennis balls while talking with Martina. Martina seemed to really like Skrimp a lot. Fizz was glad when the bus arrived across the street.

"Gotta go, guys." Skrimp said.

"Too bad," thought Fizz.

Fizz was glad when he saw Skrimp being carried away on the yellow school bus.

"Fizz?" Martina asked quietly.

"What?"

"Do you think all school buses turn into camp buses in the summer?"

"I don't know. Maybe. I'm really not sure. I don't ride the bus to school. I walk."

"I forgot."

"Doesn't your mom take you to school?"

"Yeah, a lot, even though she's really busy with work."

A bird flew down and landed on the grass in front of them and poked at the earth with her beak. Suddenly, she pulled out a reddish worm and chomped a firmer hold on it before flying up and away to her freshly hatched family.

Martina looked at Fizz. Somehow she knew he was thinking of Scamper. He had that sad look on his face. She reached over and put a hand on his shoulder. "We'll find him. I promise."

Chapter 10
Footprints

The orange afternoon sky melted into a purple-black evening sky. Fizz turned on the lamp next to his chair. He looked at the animals who were snoozing peacefully at his feet. Although he loved each and every one of them, he still missed Scamper. Martina walked into the room and flopped on the couch.

"Martina, do you think Scamper could be dead?"

"Fizz! No way! That's the kind of thinking that'll keep us from finding Scamper."

"Well, a big kid dropped in today and he said Scamper was probably run over by a car during the rainstorm."

Martina looked mad. "Who *was* this kid?"

"Trump."

"*Trump*? And you *believed* him? Fizz, he's a bully. He just wanted to get you worried."

Then Martina's eyes grew large. "Maybe it was *Trump*! It's just like him to pull a stunt like this." Her eyes grew smaller. "If only we had proof. I wish Budge hadn't washed those footprints from the hallway. We could've measured the footprints and tried to match them with someone in town."

"That's it! The hallway! Budge cleaned the *hallway*." Fizz jumped from his chair nearly landing on two cats. "But knowing how lazy Budge is, I bet he didn't clean the back stairs."

Martina was impressed by Fizz's thinking. They ran to the back steps that led down to the back door of the resort. They grabbed a ruler on the way.

Carefully, they searched every dirty step. Most of the prints belonged to their own feet. There was a set of big footprints but they were very smudgy.

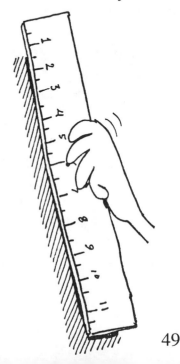

"Look, Martina! A perfect print." It was big. They laid the ruler next to it. It was exactly as long as the ruler.

"12 inches! Now all we have to do is measure everybody's feet in town."

Martina thought out loud as she walked down the steps. "Let's meet at Virginia's at eight tomorrow morning. Maybe she can give us some paper to trace people's feet. Artists always have lots of paper hanging around."

Fizz put the ruler in his secret inside coat pocket. He followed Martina outside and looked out over the sleepy town of Blue Falls. They both stood quietly for a moment. Fizz often stared out and wondered about life. One night he imagined a special library he'd like to build. It would only contain Blue Falls biographies. Everyone in town would have a book written about them. Mr. Barney's Life Story. The Adventures of Farmer Casey. Discovering Space with Martina's Mom.

But tonight all he could think about was a twelve inch pair of feet. The feet that belonged to the person who stole Scamper.

51

Chapter 11

Itching to Jump

(This next chapter is from Fizz. He has a diary, sort of. Actually it's his tape recorder. He talks to it every night. He said it was okay for us to hear because, although it was a very interesting day, it didn't have any of the real personal stuff that often he shared with T.R., his tape recorder.)

"Hi, T.R. It's me... Fizz. It's Tuesday night.

Uncle Q was nice to me tonight. He left me cheese and corn stew on the table. It was cold, but I was really hungry. Uncle Q is sleeping on the couch. He's been doing that a lot lately. His baseball team isn't doing very well. It makes him really grumpy. He gets loud when he's grumpy, so I keep out of his way. It's cool that he left cheese and corn stew for me. . . unless, maybe, he just didn't eat *his*.

Anyway, I've got to talk fast. I'm really itchy. I'll tell you why in a second.

This morning we went over to Virginia's. She's our art teacher. She was out in the backyard painting. You'll never guess whose picture she was painting. Budge's. Budge Callous. Budge had asked Virginia to paint his portrait, so he could give it as a birthday present to Elmyna Elmoy, his girlfriend.

Am I talking too fast? Oww. My arms itch.

Anyway, so we asked them both if they wanted to help us measure feet. They looked at us kinda funny. It took a while to explain what we were talking about. I thanked Budge for not cleaning the back steps. Virginia gave us paper and we all went to town.

Here's the dumb part.

I suggested a short cut to town. Well, we went across a field and came to a stone wall COVERED in poison ivy. Budge, the big show-off, said he could jump over it. He jumped it easy and stood on the other side smiling.

Virginia's long legs made jumping over the poison ivy easy.

I let Martina go next. She loves challenges. She jumped and the tip of her sneakers brushed up against the poison ivy.

I realized I wasn't going to make it. Sometimes, when I get nervous, I don't think clearly, so, well, I went to the wall and pulled off the poison ivy so my feet wouldn't touch it when I jumped over. I realized my mistake after I had an armful of poison ivy. Instead of laughing at me, Budge picked me up by the back of my jacket and ran me to a nearby stream. I was able to wash a bunch of the poison ivy off, but I'm still really itchy.

The itch didn't start until later in the afternoon, so we had time to measure feet. We counted ten people with eleven inch feet. Thirty with ten inch feet. Twenty two with nine. . . I guess the important part is this: *nobody* had a twelve inch foot. We'll keep searching. By the way, Martina said she's going to put the foot measuring data into a graph program on the computer. Mrs. Stearns, our math teacher, wrote it.

Oww. I'm too itchy to talk. Later T.R. This is Fizz. Over and Out."

Chapter 12
Trump's Pup

"According to my list, Fizz, we've measured everybody's shoe size in town."

Fizz and Martina walked slowly through the center of Blue Falls. They sat down on their favorite bench at the bus stop. Fizz looked across the street and saw a man slumped over, leaning against the big circus billboard. The man wore a straw hat.

"Farmer Casey!"

They crossed the empty street and went to Farmer Casey's side.

Fizz sat down next to him. "Are you all right?"

"No. I'm terrible. I should never have let that circus come onto my farm. Trouble. Nothin' but trouble.

And now Mr. Crumple has stopped paying me. He says he's donating the money to a worthy cause."

Martina sat down next to the farmer. "He stopped giving you half the money he makes?"

"Well, he's giving me *things* instead of money. He gave me a rusty, broken cage which I have no use for. And he gave me these dirty old boots which are much too big for me. They keep slipping off."

"Sir, can I measure those boots?" Martina asked. Fizz pulled the ruler out and handed it to Martina.

"What are you kids up to?" Farmer Casey looked confused.

Before Martina could put ruler to foot, a loud yelling and screaming interrupted them.

It was Trump, the bully. He was really upset about something. He ran up to them and yelled, "Okay.

Who's the wiseguy who stole my dog's pup?" Trump gave Fizz a mean look. "My dog, Butcher, is *really* upset. I figured it was you, Fizz, who stole the pup because of what I said to you. I was just joking around about your dog being run over by a car." He grabbed Fizz by the sweater.

Martina jumped between them. "Leave Fizz alone, Trump. He didn't take your pup. A lot of weird stuff has been going on around here and I have a feeling I know who is responsible."

Trump, Fizz and Farmer Casey stared at her.

"I think it was Mr. Crumple." She wasn't *really* sure if it was Mr. Crumple, but she figured it would get Trump to leave Fizz alone. "Let's go to the circus right now, and I bet you we'll find Trump's pup. . . and maybe Scamper!"

They tried to keep up with Martina who ran ahead of them.

Farmer Casey was getting further and further behind the group because his boots kept slipping off. Finally, he took them off and flung them as far as he could. "I can run faster barefoot."

As Farmer Casey, Trump, Fizz and Martina ran off, Farmer Casey's boots lay among some rocks by the side of the road. (Actually, they were Mr. Crumple's, weren't they?) It wasn't long before a red snake with green stripes slithered into one of the boots. It had found the perfect home.

Chapter 13
The Pow-Wow

Trump heard the little howl first. He stopped suddenly and listened.

"My pup, I can hear him."

"But we're still a mile from the circus! How could you hear him?" Fizz gasped. Fizz was glad they had stopped so he could catch his breath.

Trump pushed his way through a thorny bush and there, on the other side, at the foot of a tree, was his pup.

"Martina," Trump sneered, "you were wrong about Mr. Crumple stealing him. My pup just wandered off by himself. You know, you can get in BIG trouble accusing people of kidnapping." Trump

hugged his pup and walked off without saying
another word.

Farmer Casey said, "You know kids, Trump
may be a bully, but he *does* have a point. You can't
go around pointing fingers at people without proof."

"Those boots Mr. Crumple gave you might give
us the proof we need. If they measure twelve
inches, then we have our proof that HE stole Scamper!" Suddenly, Martina noticed that Farmer Casey
was barefoot. "Hey! Where are the boots?"

"I chucked them way back along the road."

"Come on, Fizz! We've got to find those boots."

They ran back along the road searching,

60

but Fizz and Martina never found the boots or, luckily, and the poisonous guest who had made them home.

Thick grey clouds poured slowly across the blue sky as they walked to the pet resort.

"Martina? Do you think we're in for another big storm?"

"Could be. All the more reason to call a Pow-Wow with the resort animals. We need to work fast. It'll be impossible to find Scamper if a storm like the last one hits us."

When they finally arrived at the Resort, Martina made an announcement over the loudspeaker asking all the animals to gather in the lobby. Fizz put Tony, Tammy, and Sammy in a fishbowl and brought them to the meeting. There were  cats, birds, goats and mice sitting on and under chairs. Three horses stuck their heads in through open windows. Laurel, the squirrel monkey, was busy passing out snacks for the group. She was offering grapes and cartons of milk. It was quite a scene.

"The reason I've called you here. . . " Martina

said in a commanding voice, ". . . is to ask everyone to brainstorm about how to find Scamper. I have a feeling Mr. Crumple and his circus are involved, but we need proof."

Sammy jumped out from the goldfish bowl long enough to say, "We'll do what we can to help!"

Fizz felt the jug in his hand being tugged away from him. It was Laurel.

"Hey, I'm not finished yet." He looked at the wall and noticed that Laurel

had been collecting the empty jugs and was stacking them up against the wall. "Laurel? What are you doing?"

"Sorry, Fizz. Just reeeeeecycling, see? Gettin' a count of how many we've gone through," she squealed.

"Well, that's nice, but we need your energy to find Scamper."

"I'll do some reeeeesearch. I'll reeeead up on the subject. I'll swing over to the library tomorrow."

Martina cleared her throat loudly. "Excuse me, Fizz and Laurel. We need every one's attention if we're ever going to find Scamper."

She spent the rest of the evening showing maps, photographs, pie charts, bar and line graphs to everybody. Fizz and the animals were impressed

by Martina's presentation. They were all too busy
brainstorming to notice the strong wind blowing
through the open windows until a particularly
feisty gust knocked Laurel's jug tower over. The
startled animals scurried in every direction.

Fizz wasn't sure why exactly, but he was begin-
ning to get really worried.

Chapter 14
Bananas and Books

Laurel swung from the oak tree to the slender birch just outside the Blue Falls Library. Before hopping through the window, she looked up at the sky. Thick grey clouds hovered above. The wind was blowing steadily.

In a classic squirrel monkey move, Laurel leapt from the tree, through the open window, and landed on a bookcase. She scurried to a place where no one could see her. She knew that the librarian didn't like animals in the library, so she had to do her research quietly.

Mr. Caster, the librarian, noticed that a breeze coming through an open window was blowing papers around. He closed the window and disappeared around the corner.

"Oh, brother! Now how am I going to get out, out, out?" Laurel squealed to herself.

She decided to worry about that later. First she had to read some books that might help Fizz find Scamper. She looked for a book titled "How to Find Missing Dogs," but couldn't find it. After an hour of using the computer and microfilm, Laurel found three newspaper articles written about Mr. Crumple's circus.

"Hmmm. Very interesting!"

She read carefully. In each city he visited, he had left suddenly without saying a word. And in each city his circus seemed to contain more animals.

"Curious. *Very* curious. That fellow is probably stealing animals everywhere he goes. Before we know it he could take all of us animals and — POOF ! — be gone from Blue Falls. Gotta be quick."

Laurel made photocopies of the articles. She held on to them tightly in her mouth as she hopped from one bookcase to another looking for a way out of the library. She stopped for a moment when she heard excited voices. Below her, sitting at a table, were two school children.

"I've definitely been reading a lot lately. I read a book every day last week."

"Well, so did I, except I read *two* books on Saturday and *three* on Sunday."

Laurel was glad to see some kids who liked reading so much. She, herself, was an avid reader.

Suddenly the library went dark! Completely black. Well, it seemed that way to Laurel who realized too late that someone had thrown a burlap bag over her. She had been caught. But by who?

Chapter 15

A Tree Grows in Blue Falls

Martina knocked on the door again. It opened and there was Uncle Q. He didn't say a word. In fact, he wasn't even looking at Martina. His head was twisted to his left. Martina could hear the sounds of the television and realized that Uncle Q was still watching it. Martina cleared her throat.

"Excuse me, sir. Is Fizz around?"

Uncle Q snapped out of his TV trance long enough to realize that he had opened the door. He looked down and saw Martina.

"Oh, it's you," Uncle Q said. Martina followed him inside.

Fizz walked into the living room and found

Martina and Uncle Q sitting glued to the TV set.

"Fizz, check this out! Look who's on Minimood's Express."

Fizz sat down. There on the screen was Mr. Minimood talking with a man in a top hat. It was Mr. Crumple.

Uncle Q explained, "They've been advertising this show all day. They're gonna show a rare, never-before-seen, actual monster."

Mr. Crumple stood beside a cage with a red velvet cloth draped over it. The music died down and drums began beating loudly. Everyone in the audience held their breath. Mr. Crumple yanked the red cloth off and there behind the bars of the rusty cage was. . .

"The Fabulous Feathered Fargle!" yelled Mr. Crumple.

Mr. Minimood was afraid to go near the cage.

"He won't bite you. Don't worry!" Mr. Crumple laughed as he pushed Mr. Minimood closer to the cage. "In fact, he CAN'T bite you. I've put a muzzle around the Fargle's snout so it can't open its mouth."

"Seems cruel, don't you think, Fizz?" Martina said.

"Yeah. Poor thing."

"You kids are soft, ya know that?" Uncle Q blurted out. "This Fargle monster is probably very dangerous. It probably has long fanged teeth. This Crumple guy is just thinking of everybody's safety."

When the show ended Uncle Q got up to leave.

"Fizz, I gotta go coach my no-good, rotten, stinkin' baseball team."

"I wonder why they keep losing when they have such a caring, inspirational leader?" whispered Martina.

Fizz walked over to the TV and turned it off. He picked up the plant that had been sitting on top of the set and brought it into the kitchen. Martina followed him.

"Could you make some room on the table for me?"

Martina pushed an assortment of plates, bottles, glasses and dirty napkins to one side of the table. Fizz set the plant down.

"What's with the plant, Fizz?"

"I planted a bean seed in this pot earlier this summer. The day after Scamp disappeared it started peaking out of the soil. It was like a sign, you know? Like there's hope."

"Look at how much hope you've got there, Fizz."

They stared at the strong dark green vine wrapping its way around a thin stick. Its leaves were wide and outstretched.

"I think tomorrow I'll transplant it into the garden at the Pet Resort.

Sort of a Scamper Memorial Garden."

"Fizz, relax. We'll find Scamper. A bunch of the animals are helping us out. Laurel said she was going to the library. The mice are going to snoop around at the circus tomorrow.

Fizz looked at Martina. He was getting tired of looking hopeful.

"Fizz. Trust me. You take care of your plant, and tomorrow I'll fill you in on my own top secret plan to find Scamper."

"Why do I have to wait till tomorrow?"

"Trust me, Fizz. If I told you now you'd get so nervous you wouldn't be able to sleep a wink tonight."

Fizz hardly slept a wink that night anyway.

Chapter 16
Fizz Gets a Job

Fizz found Uncle Q asleep on the couch the next morning. "Uncle Q must have lost another game," he thought as he stepped quietly into the kitchen.

Fizz grabbed a frozen bagel from the freezer for breakfast, picked up his bean plant and headed out the back door. The morning air was grey and unusually cold. As he jogged to the resort, he noticed the sky. The clouds had booked a return engagement. The wind picked up, and it made a howling noise in Fizz's ears as he ran.

Martina found Fizz in the resort garden. He had just finished planting the bean plant.

"Come inside, Fizz. I've got some hot chocolate

for you."

Martina opened the thermos and poured out the creamy cocoa into cups. Fizz sat down and took a cup.

"Isn't it weird that it's cold enough to be drinking hot cocoa in the middle of summer?"

"Fizz, this has been one of the weirdest summers I've ever experienced in my entire life. But you know — I like weird."

"No, Martina. You LOVE weird."

"Yeah, you're right. Weird isn't boring. Which leads me to your assignment."

"My what?"

"Your job. You're going to get a job with the circus."

"I've already got a job here."

"Fizz. You're going to work for the circus—not for the money — but to find out what's going on there."

By lunchtime, Fizz was at the circus. He held the ad that Martina had cut out of the newspaper. Fizz looked at his hand. It was shaking. He remembered what Martina had told him, so he closed his eyes and thought of Scamper. Suddenly, he felt braver. He knocked on the door of Mr. Crumple's trailer. The door opened slowly. A greenish-yellow face peered out at Fizz.

Fizz took a deep breath. "I'm . . . I'm . . . here about the job."

Mr. Crumple smiled. "You're hired."

74

Chapter 17
Slice of Pizza

Martina was glad that Fizz was working in the pizza trailer at the circus. It kept him busy. She decided not to worry Fizz with the news that Laurel was missing. Hopefully Fizz would find Scamper soon and perhaps Laurel.

Martina, Budge and Virginia arrived at the circus and headed straight for the pizza trailer. There weren't many people around. The cold and cloudy weather was probably to blame.

"Excuse me, sir. We'd like three slices, please."

"Hi, Martina." Fizz quickly took off his chef's hat. "Hi, Budge, Virginia. Do you guys really want some pizza?"

Budge was licking his lips. He looked like he could eat the entire pizza trailer.

"Fizz, we're not here to eat. We want to know what you've found out." Martina pulled an apple out of her pocket and handed it to Budge. He smiled for a second, but he still looked like he could eat the entire pizza trailer.

Fizz suddenly grabbed the rag and started to polish the counter furiously. He whispered, "Don't act weird. Mr. Crumple's coming over here. I'll meet you guys behind the ferris wheel after I'm done."

As Mr. Crumple got nearer, the wind suddenly picked up and knocked Fizz's glass tip jar over and the single dollar inside flew into the air. Mr. Crumple's arm shot out like a rattlesnake, grabbing the dollar from the wind. He stuffed it quickly into his velvet coat.

"Have you noticed you have customers?" said Mr. Crumple. "It's bad business for them to see you cleaning," he continued in a whisper. "They might think my circus is dirty." He laughed.

Fizz swirled around fast and pulled a pizza off the warming rack. He handed slices to his friends. Budge was delighted. They paid and slipped away.

Mr. Crumple ran his long, bony finger along the greasy counter. "Can you work late tomorrow night, Fizz? I need help taking the tents down. There seems to be a storm heading this way. Time to move on, I guess."

Fizz was speechless. Mr. Crumple rubbed his wiry chin with his scarred hands.

"I'd also like to talk to you about a long-term employment opportunity."

"Pardon me, sir?" Fizz gulped.

Mr. Crumple leaned toward Fizz. "Pack up your things and come work for me. Just think. . . all the pizza you can eat and *four* dollars a day. No more uncle *bossing* you around. Think about it."

Mr. Crumple spun around and marched across the windy field toward his trailer.

Chapter 18
The Meeting

At six o'clock, Fizz closed up. He hadn't sold a slice in hours. It wasn't until he stepped outside the warm pizza trailer that he noticed how cold it had become. A light drizzle was falling.

"No wonder there's hardly anyone here," Fizz thought to himself as he ran to the ferris wheel.

"Fizz! Over here!"

It was Martina's voice coming from behind a large wooden box. Fizz found his friends and began talking quickly.

"We don't have much time. Crumple's ready to pack up the circus and move out of town. And if I'm not careful, he's going to take *me* with him."

"Did you find your dog?" asked Budge.

"No, but I've snuck into almost every tent and I was able to talk to a lot of the animals. They're miserable. They want me, I mean, *us* to help them escape."

"Did you talk to the Feathered Fargle?" asked Martina.

"No, Mr. Crumple was guarding that tent."

Rain began falling faster.

"I've got an idea," said Budge in his deep voice. "Mr. Crumple will be in his trailer while it rains. We can each pick a tent and free the animals."

"We can put them in Farmer Casey's barn," suggested Fizz.

"Okay. Let's go," Martina said. "Budge, you take the green tent. Fizz, you take the yellow tent. Virginia, how about the purple tent?"

"Well, actually it's not purple. It's really mauve," Virginia explained. "But I *do* love that color."

"Mauve is my favorite color," said Fizz. "Actually, it's my lucky color. Maybe I should take the mauve tent."

Virginia paused a moment.

"Hmm. I guess mauve is *my* favorite color, too."

Budge said, "Virginia, I thought you told me

79

every color was your favorite color."

"Did I say that? I agree with myself, but if I could only choose *one* color to, say, paint my house it would be mauve. Or something in the purple family."

"I'm sorry to break up this fascinating discussion," interrupted Martina, "but we've got a job to do."

Chapter 19

Feathers

Thunder clobbered noisily in the darkness of the rainy night. Fizz ran across the muddy field to the mauve tent. (Virginia had ended up volunteering to rescue the red tent.) Through the downpour, Fizz could see Martina escorting six horses and two small monkeys towards Farmer Casey's barn. He took a deep breath and slipped into the tent. The Fargle was asleep in its cage. Its wings were still sticking out as though it were in flight. Fizz noticed the muzzle was not on the Fargle's mouth.

"I hope this thing doesn't bite. Maybe I'll just open the cage and run. . ."

He crept toward the cage and slowly reached

toward the rusty bolt that kept the cage door shut.

"Here goes!" He closed his eyes and yanked the bolt out. The cage door swung open with a large squeak. The Feathered Fargle's eyes shot open! The Fargle shook its head and looked ready to jump.

Fizz headed for the door of the tent as quickly as he could. He ran into the stormy field and headed straight for the barn. The Fargle leapt from its cage and dashed through the tent door into the pouring rain. Fizz turned his head just long enough to see the Fargle racing across the field toward him. The Fargle's wings were outstretched. Fizz was terrified. He tried to run faster.

He wanted to yell for help, but he knew Mr. Crumple might hear, so he just kept running. The barn was only a few yards away when Fizz slipped in a deep puddle landing him flat on his back.

The Fargle jumped on top of Fizz and. . . began licking his face! The Fargle surprised Fizz by growling in a low, but friendly voice "It's me! Your dog! Scamper!"

Fizz opened his eyes to see that the soggy feathered thing really was his long lost dog.

Scamper's feathered ear suddenly shot straight up. Fizz heard the strange, angry howl too. "Was that a coyote, Scamp?"

"No, it's Mr. Crumple. He sounds mad."

"Quick, let's go."

The rain soaked them as they made it to the barn, slipped inside and shut the barn door. Budge and Martina were surprised to see Fizz holding the soggy Feathered Fargle.

"It's Scamp! I found him! Mr. Crumple glued *chicken feathers* to him and tied *wings* onto him!"

The barn was filled with the sounds of Farmer Casey's animals and their new guests from the circus.

"Where's Virginia?"

"She'll be back soon. She went to get help from Farmer Casey and Chief Blinker," Martina explained.

Fizz noticed Laurel, the squirrel monkey, sitting on Budge's shoulder.

"Why do you have a clown suit on, Laurel?"

"It's a long story. A lonnggg story."

"Hey," growled Scamper, "Would you guys mind taking these feathers off me. I'd *love* to look like the dog I once was."

It was a long night. Fizz spent hours removing all the feathers from Scamper. Budge and Virginia removed all the tight collars from the circus animals. Farmer Casey and Martina cooked everyone up a late night snack. Chief Blinker took Mr. Crumple away on a number of charges (stealing animals, false advertising, cruelty to animals). Finally, Uncle Q and Martina's mom and dad arrived.

Farmer Casey promised to drive the circus animals over to the resort the next day.

Fizz curled up with Scamper in the back of Uncle Q's car and fell asleep. As Uncle Q drove them home, he noticed a warm breeze blowing.

The clouds parted and a beam of moonlight fell upon the sleepy town of Blue Falls.

Chapter 20
The Party

Fizz woke to a summer breeze blowing through an open window. He felt Scamper sprawled out over his legs like a comforter.

"Hey, Scamp. Are you awake?"

"No," he growled softly with his eyes shut tight.

"Oh. Well, let me know when you are."

One of Scamper's ears moved slightly upward. "One of my ears is awake, so you can talk to me."

"Scamp, I just wanted to say it's great to have you home and that I'm really sorry I didn't find you sooner."Fizz sat up and rubbed his dog behind the ear. Scamper smiled.

"Just keep scratching, and I'll forget that the

whole summer happened."

Fizz scratched while Scamper forgot. Fizz gently plucked the last few feathers still clinging to Scamper's fur. They were interrupted by Uncle Q's loud voice booming from downstairs.

"Fizz! Get down here! And bring your mutt with you! Move it!"

"Boy. We barely got a chance to relax and he's bossing us around." Fizz slipped on his ratty slippers, threw on his plaid bathrobe and stumbled toward the door. Scamper trotted behind him.

They walked into the kitchen where Uncle Q stood with his back toward them.

"Uncle Q? What's the matter?"

Uncle Q spun around with a huge plate of pancakes dripping with butter and maple syrup. He had a big smile on his big face. "Sit down and eat. I hate it when food gets cold."

Uncle Q threw a couple of pancakes into Scamper's bowl. Fizz sat at the table trying not to look too surprised. His uncle flipped a couple of pancakes onto Fizz's plate. The pancakes were in the shape of animals!

"I figured you guys have been through a lot, so I made special pancakes for you and Scamp. I made Scamp's in the shape of bones."

"Wow! Uncle Q! You. . . you're. . . "

"Don't get goofy on me. Just eat your breakfast. You can thank me by doing the dishes and cleaning the frying pan. I've got to get to the stadium.

My team won a double-header last night. I've got to make sure these guys keep on their toes for tonight's game." He put on his cap and opened the back door. "By the way, if you want to go to tonight's game just drop by the ticket office."

"Thanks, Uncle Q, but Martina and I are planning on having a party at the resort later. . . "

"Whatever." Uncle Q left out the back door.

Later on, Fizz and Scamper went down to the pet resort. They found their special guests from the circus already relaxing and meeting the other animals. Some of the animals still looked shaken up. Martina was explaining to them that they were free to come and go as they pleased.

Martina noticed Fizz and Scamper. "Fizz! Scamp!" Martina ran over and hugged Scamper. Within seconds, Scamper was surrounded. Martina and Fizz stepped away from the cheering animals so they could hear each other.

"Fizz, we did it! Now we can enjoy the rest of the summer in peace and, well, maybe not quiet." They looked over at the crowd of squeaking, chirping, barking animals.

"Fizz, about the party. . . Can you pick up some snacks at the store?"

Fizz remembered that he still had money in his pocket from his pizza job. He counted the money. "Hey! I've still got eight dollars from my job."

"See, Fizz. Everything happens for a reason."

Fizz smiled as he walked away.

He borrowed Budge's bike and went to the Shop N' Spend store nearby. He loaded up with as many party supplies as eight dollars could buy.

The fellow at the cash register smiled at Fizz.

"Having a party, son?"

"Yes, sir. A celebration."

"What are you celebrating?"

"Sir, it's a long story. A lonnnnnnnnng story."

More about
Fizz & Martina and Friends

Fizz and Martina are the stars of a video series called "The Wonderful Problems of Fizz & Martina." Their adventures unfold in many episodes while presenting math problems for kids to talk about and solve together. If you haven't seen the series, here's a little background information.

Fizz

His name is Fizzmond, but his friends call him Fizz. He's a bit nervous and shy. Living with his Uncle Quesmit isn't always easy, but he tries hard to be positive and get the most out of life. He likes sharing his ideas and dreams with his best friend, Martina, and T.R., his tape recorder.

Martina

She's brave, creative and always ready for adventure. She lives on a little island in southern Blue Falls. Her mom and dad are both astronomers, although her Mom also runs a worm farm, and her dad writes cook books.

Budge

He's big. He's olive green. He looks scary, but he's quite a nice guy if you give him half a chance. Baseball is his favorite sport. Budge also enjoys lifting heavy things. Fizz and Martina have never actually seen Budge's parents and wonder sometimes why he never talks about them.

Virginia

Art classes at Blue Falls School haven't been the same since Virginia joined the staff. She believes that every student is an artist; that every color is beautiful; that plaid and polka-dots match. She lives in her art studio along Blue Falls River.

Uncle Q

It was a shock to Uncle Q when he had to take Fizz into his home. Uncle Q doesn't really like taking care of anything, except his baseball team, The Blue Falls Dingers. The Q stands for Quesmit. He loves his red sports car, watching television (especially sporting events.) The list of things that annoy him is too long to print here.

Mr. Barney

He is Fizz and Martina's math teacher at Blue
Falls school. His math classes are a lot of fun because he teaches everything with a story. And what
a great storyteller he is! During the summer, Mr.
Barney works in the ice cream store he owns in
downtown Blue Falls.